Family Story Collection

Always Follow Your Heart

Stories About Family, Love, and Friendship

Book Two

Printed in China
First Edition
1 3 5 7 9 10 8 6 4 2

ISBN 0-7868-3526-5

For more Disney Press fun, visit www.disneybooks.com

Book Two

———∞∞∞———

Always Follow
Your Heart

———∞∞∞———

STORIES ABOUT FAMILY, LOVE, AND FRIENDSHIP

Introduction

True love sometimes requires courage—the courage to love someone who is different, the courage to wait for love, and the courage not to settle for less. Love may not always come easily, but when the obstacles have been conquered and the trials have been passed, the joy of togetherness makes everything worthwhile. When you follow your heart, you are seldom misguided.

In "Silly, Romantic Ideas," the Prince knows that the throne will have no meaning unless he can share it with someone he truly loves. His patience is rewarded in the end with Cinderella's heart and hand in marriage. Similarly, in "A Prized Kiss," Maid Marian gives up a life of wealth and privilege once she realizes that only the love of her childhood sweetheart, Robin Hood, will bring her real happiness.

Silly, Romantic Ideas

from *Cinderella*

Follow your heart, no matter what others may say.

"It's time that my son got married and settled down," the King said to the Grand Duke.

"Now, now," the Grand Duke said, comforting the King. "Perhaps if we just let him alone—"

"Let him alone?" the King interrupted. "Him and his silly, romantic ideas?"

"But, Sire, in matters of love—" the Grand Duke began.

"Ha! What is love?" the King scoffed. "Just a

boy meeting a girl under the right conditions. We must simply arrange those conditions."

The King decided to hold a ball and invite every maiden in the kingdom. He sent messengers to deliver the invitations. One of the many eligible maidens who received an invitation was a young woman named Cinderella.

Meanwhile, the Prince learned of the plans. Didn't his father understand? Meeting a young lady was not the problem—it was meeting a *special* one, someone who would make his heart flutter.

Still, he agreed to attend the ball. That night, as one young lady after another came in and curtsied, the Prince grew bored. Would this evening ever end?

But then, from across the room, he noticed

another maiden. She was beautiful, but there was something more—something that made him push past the other young ladies to get closer to her.

As the Prince approached the beautiful maiden, he felt his heart flutter. Yes, this one is special, he thought.

The Prince and the young woman danced without saying a word. They gazed at each other, not needing to speak. So this is what

everyone always talks about, the Prince thought. This is love.

As the clock started to chime, the young lady suddenly gasped and pulled away. "It's midnight!" she cried. "Good-bye . . ."

"Wait! Please come back!" the Prince cried, chasing after her. "I don't even know your name!"

A moment later, the maiden was gone, leaving behind only a single glass slipper that she had lost in her haste.

The Prince was heartbroken. Just when he had finally found love, it had slipped through his fingers.

His father was still eager to see him married, so he ordered the Grand Duke to try the glass slipper on every maiden in the kingdom. The Prince would marry the one it fit.

The Grand Duke, with help from the footman, tried the slipper on one lady after another, but to no avail. Finally, they reached the last house in the kingdom. It was Cinderella's house. First, the footman tried the glass slipper on her stepsisters, but no matter how hard they each tried to squeeze their foot into the slipper, it just didn't fit.

As the Grand Duke and the footman were about to leave, Cinderella appeared.

"May I try on the slipper?" she asked.

As the footman approached Cinderella, her angry stepmother tripped him. The glass slipper shattered into pieces.

"Oh, no!" cried the Grand Duke.

"But you see, I have the other slipper," said Cinderella.

She gently slid her foot inside the slipper.

It was a perfect fit. Cinderella was the Prince's true love.

At once, the King arranged the wedding. He didn't want the Prince's dream girl to slip away again!

He need not have worried. Neither the Prince nor Cinderella had any intention of ever losing each other again.

A Prized Kiss

from *Robin Hood*

No matter how large the divide, love can bridge the gap.

Deep in Sherwood Forest, Robin Hood and Little John were tending to their chores, but Robin's mind kept wandering. He was daydreaming about Maid Marian, his true love.

Growing up, Robin Hood and Maid Marian had been sweethearts. But now they had very different lives. Maid Marian lived at the castle with her uncle, greedy Prince John, while Robin Hood and his band of Merry Men lived as outlaws in Sherwood Forest, robbing from the rich to feed the poor of Nottingham.

"Why don't you stop mopin' around and marry the girl?" Little John said to Robin Hood.

"Marry her?" Robin Hood replied. "You don't just walk up to a girl and say, 'Hey, remember me? Will you marry me?' It just isn't done that way."

As much as Robin Hood loved Maid Marian, he was not sure they had a future together.

Still, when Robin Hood learned that the evil Prince John was hosting an archery tournament, and that the winner would get a kiss from Maid Marian, Robin Hood entered right away. He and Little John decided to dress in disguise so that Prince John would not recognize them.

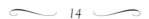

At the tournament, Robin Hood, dressed like a stork, walked up to the royal box, and handed a flower to Maid Marian. "It is a

great honor to be shootin' for the favor of a lovely lady like yourself," he said. "I hope I win the kiss."

Maid Marian was certain that the stork was actually her beloved Robin Hood. She watched with delight as he handily won the

archery tournament.

Then Robin Hood stood before the royal box to collect his prize. He did not know that Prince John had discovered his true identity as well and was setting a trap to catch him.

"Archer," said Prince John. "I commend you, and because of your superior skill, you shall get what is coming to you." With a sweep of his sword, Prince John cut off Robin Hood's disguise. "Seize him!" he shouted.

The guards tied up Robin Hood while Maid Marian pleaded with Prince John. "Please, have mercy," she begged.

"My dear, emotional lady," the Prince replied. "Why should I?"

"Because . . . I love him, Your Highness," Maid Marian explained.

Prince John would not listen, but Marian's words were music to Robin Hood's ears!

With Little John's help, Robin Hood managed to escape. Then, with the guards hot on his heels, Robin Hood swung in on a vine and swept Maid Marian off her feet— and onto the top of the royal box.

"Marian, my love," Robin Hood said, "will you marry me?"

Marian smiled. "Oh, darling, I thought you'd never ask!"

Together they escaped to Sherwood Forest, where Robin Hood gave Maid Marian an engagement ring made of flowers. At that moment, their lives did not seem very different, after all.